Snowball
the Dancing
Cockatoo

Snowball
the Dancing
Cockatoo

Sy Montgomery

With Illustrations by
Judith Oksner

Bauhan Publishing
Peterborough, New Hampshire
2013

Dedication

For McKenzie Lewis
—as I look forward to reading
your own book one day

Chapter One

"Brrrrring! Brrrrrring!"

A human would mistake the sound for a ringing phone. But I know better.

That's no telephone. It's Mitzi, the African gray parrot who lives in the cage next to mine. And I know what she'll do next, too. She'll answer it.

"Hello!" she says in a voice like a cheery old lady. *"Ohhhh! Is that so?"* Mitzi pauses as if she's listening to a caller. *"Tell me more!"* She laughs. *"Really? Oh yes, I agree, yes."* And so the conversation goes—on her imaginary phone with her imaginary caller.

Finally, Mitzi has talked long enough. *"Okay! See you Friday!"* And then she makes the click of a phone hanging up. Mitzi parrots it all perfectly. No wonder: she's a parrot.

Many of us here at Bird Lovers Only parrot rescue share Mitzi's talent. Take the African grays, Ben and Bandit, whose cages are next door to one another, right beside mine.

They used to live with an older couple. Bandit speaks in the voice of the wife:

"La-rry! Telephone!"

Ben plays the husband, Larry. *"What?"* he asks wearily. But it's not always Larry's *voice* Ben imitates. Ben usually waits till the room is silent. Then he lets loose with his masterpiece—another sound that also seems to have graced the couple's home often enough for Ben to have perfected its every note:

"Pfffffttttttttttthhhhh!"

Bandit offers his review in the voice of the wife: *"Oh, my WORD!"*

Then Ralph, the blue and gold macaw, starts up. He opens his wings and calls out, *"C'mon in!"* Mookie, a large white Moluccan cockatoo, starts in. *"BAAAA!"* Sheep used to live in her yard. Next, June, another macaw, screams, *"Cut it out! Cut it out!"*

Few parrots can resist adding to the symphony. Some of us can mimic car alarms, police sirens, dripping faucets, and barking dogs. You should hear us. We beat any composition of Mozart's, if you ask me. He wrote fine music, I'll grant you—just a bit limited. But parrots could have improved his work. To the notes he penned, we might have added, for instance, the sounds of squeaking hinges, the calls of barnyard animals—and maybe even Larry's troubled tummy.

Yes, we parrots are great composers, and great performers, too. You'd think more of us would go into show business, like I did. But I'm the first to admit that while parrots are surely the most splendid and brilliant of creatures, not every parrot is as talented as I am.

I'm a sulfur crested cockatoo—a medium-sized white parrot with a tall yellow crest. But folks around here call me a "rockatoo." That's because when I dance, I really rock out! Surely you've seen my video on You Tube: *Time* magazine named it one of the top 10 videos of the year. (You can find the web address in the back of the book.)

Since my You Tube debut, I've danced on *The Tonight Show* and on *Good Morning America*. I pooped on the back of a chair on *The Late Show*. My fame has spread far beyond my cage, way beyond my neighborhood in Schererville, Indiana—even beyond the continent of North America. Recently I starred on a quiz show in Japan. It was called *Believe or Not*. Two of the five human panelists on the program couldn't believe a bird could dance like I do.

But then, people often underestimate us parrots. People don't realize how smart we are. They don't understand how strong we are. They don't appreciate our talents.

And that's what gets us into trouble. That's what landed every one of us here at the parrot rescue. We were all abandoned by our former owners—even me.

Why would anyone give up the chance to live with someone so beautiful, so gifted? Someone who can both fly and talk, someone devoted enough to stick with a mate for life—a life that can last for seventy years or more? Go figure. We parrots suppose it must have something to do with humans' many limitations. (They're not that bright—the poor, featherless things.)

For instance, most humans don't understand parrot humor. One of my friends, an all-white Moluccan cockatoo named Angel, has a genius for solving puzzles—and the most intriguing puzzle of all is how to get out of our cages when people aren't looking. So Angel figures this out for us. No matter how many different kinds of clips or locks close our cage doors, Angel opens them with her strong beak and deft tongue. She loves to dump all the food in all the cages on the ground. It's fun hearing the dishes crash when they hit the floor—plonk!—and watching all the pellets, fruit, and nuts scatter everywhere. Whee! Then we all come out of our cages, shrieking at the tops of our lungs with pleasure, and toss our toys around and chew the furniture. Can you imagine anything more hilarious? Yet when the people finally discover Angel's merry prank, they never laugh. They just don't get it.

Chewing is another thing people don't appreciate—even when we're doing it for THEM! One parrot I know created a lovely nest for him and his person. (We parrots normally choose fellow parrots as mates, and we usually nest in hollow trees. But in captivity, we can make do.) One day while the person was out, the parrot enlarged the opening beneath an antique chest of drawers. Shredding the wood with his chisel-like beak, he created a cozy cave within the chest. He even lined the cavity with soft, chewed bedroom curtains.

It was a great nest site, believe me. You'd think the person would have been impressed. But no. The person wouldn't even go inside to inspect it, much less lay an egg there.

Alas, it was a doomed romance. His human mate couldn't measure up to parrot standards. The way I see it, parrots are superior to people in every way. But strangely, most people are so confused, they actually think it's the other way around! No wonder humans have trouble meeting the demands of such creative minds—not to mention such busy beaks. Too many captive parrots never find the homes they deserve.

Luckily for my many fans, I did. So I'd like to thank all the little people. Every great performer deserves a lucky break—and though I didn't know it at the time, the day my people brought me to Bird Lovers Only parrot rescue, I got mine. This is my story.

BIRD BASICS — PARROT PRIMER

Luckily for you humans and the rest of birdkind, more than 350 different kinds of parrots grace the Earth, from the tiny three-and-a-half-inch-long buff-faced pygmy parrot of New Guinea to the eagle-sized hyacinth macaw of South America. We parrots—including macaws, lovebirds, cockatiels, parakeets, lories, lorikeets, and, of course, the best ones of all, cockatoos like me—live wild all over the warmer parts of the globe.

Though parrots come in lots of different colors, shapes, and sizes, it's easy to recognize one of us: we all have stout, strong, hooked beaks, large heads relative to the body, and strong, muscular tongues. (We use our tongues to move stuff around and to make different sounds instead of for tasting. Birds have relatively few taste buds, and none are on the tongue; they're all on the roof and lining of our mouths.)

With two toes on each foot facing forward and two toes facing back, we parrots use our feet the way you use your hands. Watch me eat a piece of fruit: I'll hold it up in one claw before biting into it with my beak.

By using my strong parrot beak and feet, I can climb as well as most birds can fly. That makes most of us parrots quite acrobatic. We love to hang upside down, sometimes from one foot, and get into funny positions. We're lucky, too: parrots are among the longest-lived animals on earth, with some of us living up to 120 years!

Chapter Two

The day I came to Bird Lovers Only, I was in one rotten mood.

I was angry. I was scared. And my feelings were hurt. Who could blame me? That morning I'd woken up in my cage as usual—only to be stuffed into a travel carrier (the sort of thing people use to move a revolting CAT, no less!), carted off to a place I'd never seen before, and left there! The whole thing made me want to bite.

The other parrots tried to explain. All those conversations on nonexistent telephones, all those snatches of conversation—they are all spoken snapshots of the homes they left behind. But I didn't want to listen. It was a few hours before I truly understood what had happened: My family didn't want me anymore.

And it was all the humans' fault. I'd been betrayed!

Maybe I should have known better from the start.

And it all started because I was unlucky in love. Admittedly, we were a star-crossed

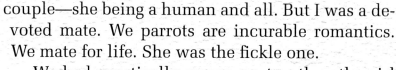

couple—she being a human and all. But I was a devoted mate. We parrots are incurable romantics. We mate for life. She was the fickle one.

We had practically grown up together, the girl and I, in a nice suburban home with a loving mom and dad. Then one day, as I reached the brink of young adult parrothood (as in many things, we cockatoos are ahead of humans in the maturity department, and become adults between the ages of five and seven), I realized the girl was more than just a friend. She was the love of my life.

Okay, she was the only unmated female around. In the wild, cockatoos live in a flock of a hundred birds or more. A handsome guy like me would have my pick of the ladies. But the dating scene is limited if you're living in the suburbs in a cage.

Sure, I had hatched from an egg and alas—she couldn't help it—she was a mammal. It wasn't her fault she was covered in skin instead of feathers, or that she had no wings. We had other things in common. Music, for instance. We shared a love of the rock group the Backstreet Boys. It was her dad's favorite band, too. He'd slip a shiny disc into the CD player and turn it up really loud. I'd bob my head. She'd bob hers.

I'd raise a claw. She'd raise an arm. I'd toss my crest. She'd toss her hair. Those were the days.

But then one day, the girl betrayed me. At first, I didn't know what happened. All I knew was, she just disappeared.

I sulked. I didn't want to eat. It was enough to make you want to pull your own feathers out! You see, while a cockatoo might fly off alone for a little while (sometimes you need to scout a new source of fruit or nesting material), there is just no way you'd desert your mate for days on end. The first day went by, and then another. She must be lost or hurt, I worried. After a week, I resigned myself. A hawk or owl must have eaten her.

And then, one day, she walked right back through the door, as if nothing had happened. Where had she been? What disaster had intervened to cause our unbearable separation? When I found out, I was appalled. She had gone off, ON PURPOSE, to some place called "college"—and worse, she was planning to go back there again!

Naturally, I was livid. Of all the feckless, rotten, fickle—well, I just flew at her and bit her. In fact, every time I saw her or heard her voice, I'd fly at her and bite.

She ran off, screaming. The parents tried to intervene. They said I was worse than all the birds in Alfred Hitchcock. But what did they expect? She had committed an unforgiveable sin. No decent, upstanding parrot would ever do such a thing to her mate. Besides, I never bit her as hard as I could: my beak is strong enough to snap a broom handle or open a Coke can. I should have been commended for my restraint.

But no. Even the humans admit their justice is blind. I think it's blind, deaf, and just plain dumb! The parents should have taken my side. Instead—can you imagine it?—they kept their daughter and got rid of ME.

The situation was terribly unfair. So when I first got to Bird Lovers Only, I fumed. I pouted. I slicked down my feathers. I fluffed them up again. I scratched my beak with my claw. I thought awhile.

We parrots may be emotional, but we're a generally cheerful, creative lot, and we are great thinkers. If life doesn't give you fruit, you can always eat nuts. And if you don't like nuts, at least you can throw them on the floor, which is highly entertaining. Maybe I could work with this.

Maybe the move wasn't a disaster after all. It was nice to see other parrots: talkative African grays, colorful macaws, pretty Amazons, and neat little cockatiels with perky crests and orange cheeks. There were even other cockatoos, though they were both Moluccans, not sulfur cresteds like me. In other rooms on my floor, and upstairs, too, I heard lovebirds and at least one hyacinth macaw. Parrots everywhere were chatting with each other, ringing bells with their beaks, pecking at mirrors, eating nuts, snacking on fruit, and cheerfully chewing their toys to shreds.

I liked the lady who had taken me out of the carrier and put me in my cage. She sort of looked like a cockatoo herself. She had pretty, yellow, spiky hair that stood up like a crest, and shiny, gentle eyes. I noticed there was a guitar in one corner. Maybe it was hers. And in another corner, I spotted a CD player hooked up to some sizeable speakers.

Maybe, I thought, there would be music. Maybe one day I would feel like dancing again.

BIRD BASICS — HONORED THROUGH THE AGES

For our intelligence, beauty, playfulness, and ability to speak, naturally we parrots have enchanted humans for thousands of years. Pictures of parrots are carved inside the ancient tombs of Egyptian pharaohs.

In the third century BC, the famous philosopher Aristotle (smart man!) kept a parrot for company—and perhaps counsel. The Roman Emperor Caesar Augustus had a parakeet who greeted him by proclaiming "Hail, emperor!" each day. Parrots were prized throughout the Roman Empire and housed in fancy cages carved from expensive ivory and silver. (Perhaps I should discuss this decorating option with my people.)

In the seventeenth century, the English Duchess of Richmond and Lennox so loved her pet African gray that she decreed that not even death should part them. According to her wishes, after both died— the parrot shortly after the Duchess—a statue of the Duchess was fashioned out of wax, and her parrot was stuffed. They still can be seen together in Westminster Abbey.

Chapter Three

"Hello, Snowball!" the yellow-crested lady said to me. "Would you like to come out of your cage?"

Boy, would I! I almost put up my crest feathers—but I didn't want to seem too eager. Instead, I cocked my head and looked at her quizzically out of one eye. My black mood vanished. I decided not to even nip her.

When she reached in, I stepped onto her hand. I rode out the door of my cage.

"We like to give everyone here some special playtime," she explained to me in a soft, kind voice. "Maybe you'd like to try one of the parrot gyms?" She glanced toward a parrot-sized jungle gym made of PVC pipe and adorned with bells, rope, wood, rawhide and hard plastic toys.

Wow—maybe this could be fun, I thought. But just then, the lady had another idea. "I almost forgot," she said. She put me on the back of a swivel chair near her computer, while she went over to a table and pulled something out of a paper bag. "Your people left this with me," she told me. "They wouldn't say what it was, but they said to play it, and watch what happens!"

She slid a shiny disc into the CD player, and out it came: the irresistible beat of the Backstreet Boys' smash hit, "Everybody"!

My yellow crest shot up tall. Joy welled up in my cockatoo heart. Before I knew it, I was bobbing my body, stepping from foot to foot, lifting my wings and spreading my tail. I'm an artist, after all, and couldn't help myself. My muse was calling.

Every bod-y! Rock your bod-y!

I did what the lyrics demanded.

Rock your bod-y, right!

"Oh, my God!" the yellow-crested lady cried. She looked like she was going to faint. "What is going on?" She had seen birds dance—but never like this before. She called to her mate. "Chuck, come here—you've got to see this!"

I bounced and twirled and squawked. The beat was in my blood.

Music is something all parrots appreciate—though of course we all have individual tastes. Some birds prefer the high voices of female singers. Others like the delicate tunes of the classical composers. The parakeets seem to have a thing for brassy wind instruments. But hey, I ask you: is there anything that gets your crest up like rock n' roll? As I danced, other parrots were groovin' to the tune, too: I noticed Mitzi bobbing her head along to the music, and heard Angel in the back room shrieking with delight.

But I was clearly the star of the show. Besides, the lyrics of the song are obviously about me! Listen:

Got a question for you, the lead singer says. *Better answer now.*
Ye-ah! goes the chorus.
Am I original? asks the lead singer.
I particularly like to scream right there in the song. It's my favorite part. Am I original?
How many other dancing birds do you know?
Ye-ah! the chorus agrees. And so did Yellow Crest and her mate.

When the song ended, naturally the humans broke into applause. "Yay, Snowball!" they cried. I love applause—what great showman doesn't? As they clapped, I tossed my crest and bowed my head over and over. They could tell I was ready for an encore.

"Chuck, we have to film this!" the lady insisted. I agreed this was a fine idea. Her mate quickly fetched the home video cam. "Ready, Snowball?"

You bet I was! In fact, after my warm-up, I think my performance was even better the second time. I vogued for the camera. I varied my dance steps. Raise the right foot once, the left foot twice. (We cockatoos are mostly left-footed, like most people are right-handed.) Right foot once, left foot thrice. Erect the crest. Bob the head. Turn around, then back around again to face the camera. One-two-three-four, keeping the beat with every feather of my snowy white body.

When the song ended, the glorious applause sounded again. I bowed graciously.

My pounding heart soared like a parrot flying over the rainforest canopy. Finally I had found an audience worthy of my genius!

"Wow, we've got some special parrot here!" Yellow Crest said. "Wait till people see this. We're not going to have any trouble adopting HIM out!"

Adopting WHO out? I thought. Are these people nuts? Don't they recognize a star when they see one?

Clearly, staying with Bird Lovers Only was going to be crucial to launching my stage career—even though the people didn't know it yet.

BIRD BASICS — CUCKOO for COCKATOOS

There are more than forty different species of cockatoos on Earth, living wild in Australia and the nearby islands of New Guinea and Indonesia. Most cockatoos are white with tall, curling crests, like me—I happen to be a medium sulfur-crested cockatoo, the handsomest variety, if I do say so myself. But all cockatoos are remarkably attractive: Some of us, like the palm cockatoos, are black. Some, like the galahs, are mostly pink. And all of us are very smart indeed.

Sometimes that gets us in trouble. One book written for potential pet parrot owners warns that many cockatoos "can shriek with tremendous power, which restricts their popularity." Maybe it does in people's homes; but in our natural flocks, shrieking sometimes expresses our popularity!

In the wild, we cockatoos usually live in big flocks—one hundred birds or more—flying free over fifty miles each day. So you can imagine how bored someone as smart as me might get living alone in a cage all day. And many poor birds do. If you see their people, would you tell them something for me? Let them know their bird needs lots of fun, exercise, and company. Tell them you're a friend of mine.

Chapter Four

I know I already mentioned this, but it bears repeating: humans—poor flightless creatures that they are—sometimes just aren't that bright. At least not as bright as we parrots. Sometimes even when we say something to them in plain English, they still don't understand. They think we're merely "parroting." Which sometimes we are, just for fun—and sometimes we aren't. The problem is, humans don't always know how to listen.

So in order to stay at my new home, I knew I had to find a way to get the idea across that was so obvious, so clear, so unmistakable, that even PEOPLE would get it.

Fortunately, I had a brilliant Plan. It wasn't long before I had to put it into action.

The next day, Yellow Crest greeted me sweetly. "Hello, Snowball! There's somebody I want you to meet!" With her was another lady. To be honest, she looked like a perfectly nice person to me. I later found out that she was a volunteer at the parrot rescue, and thus a human of impeccable taste and high moral character. But I knew what Yellow Crest had in mind. She wanted this lady to adopt me. I vowed to stick to my Plan.

Yellow Crest took me out of my cage and carried me to perch on the back of the couch to meet the new lady. I walked across the back of the couch, as if I were ready to snuggle up to her. "Hello, Snowball!" the nice lady said.

And then I implemented my Plan.

I bit her on the ear.

"Ow! Ow!" she cried. It was a dramatic moment. Quite memorable, I would say. Blood was running down the lady's neck. Yellow Crest rushed to get her a tissue, and then ice, and then some tea, to help her recover from this horrible and gory experience.

I felt bad about hurting her; I had nothing against her, after all. But I had to stick with my Plan. I had to make sure nobody else adopted me. I tried to tell myself that really, I had done her a favor. Many people, I've noticed, get pierced ears. I did one of hers for free.

This lady, though, was not up for multiple piercings—at least not with a cockatoo beak. She knew enough about parrots to get the message: I wasn't going home with her that day. Not that day, or ever!

But Yellow Crest still felt she should try to find me another home. Perhaps she felt she didn't really deserve me. Besides, space is limited here at Bird Lovers Only. And sure, there are other parrots here that are difficult to adopt out. Bandit lost one eye to an early injury. Ben's feet can't grasp a perch properly, so he needs a special plank to sit on in his cage. Mookie has a terrible feather-picking problem. They will stay here forever. But me—I'm sure Yellow Crest figured I'd be one hot property. Who wouldn't want ME? I'd be a cinch to place.

I had to make sure that didn't happen.

So every time she introduced me to a potential adopter, I deployed the Plan. Armed with a beak that can open a nut that humans need a hammer to crack, I went for every person who showed up to adopt me.

I'm not proud of what I did. I felt badly hurting and scaring innocent people. I would never have bitten unless I had to. I created quite a scene. Words were said that Yellow Crest hoped that we parrots wouldn't pick up. Blood flowed. Quickly, the Band-Aid box was emptied. One man spent the evening holding a paper towel to his lip. Yellow Crest hovered over him, apologizing on my behalf.

It wasn't a pretty scene—but at least it was a scene! And I was the center of attention. (I have to admit, we parrots sometimes deserve our reputation as drama queens.) But most important of all, the Plan worked. Yellow Crest decided I wouldn't be adopted out, after all. I would get to stay here forever!

And that was a mighty good thing for Bird Lovers Only—because on a whim, Chuck, the mate, had posted my video on You Tube. We didn't know it, but it would be only a matter of days before my cockatoo career took wing.

BIRD BASICS — BIRDY SUPERPOWERS

Poor humans! Not only can't they fly; they can't see all the colors we birds do. You need a map and a compass to do what we birds can do in our heads.

Birds' eyes are packed with special receptors, including some kinds of receptors humans don't have at all. Humans have two kinds of receptors for color; we birds have at least three. That's proof that birds can almost surely see colors humans don't even know exist. We can see in the ultra-violet spectrum, beyond the blue and purple part of the rainbow, which people can't. In fact, to us, colors are so vibrant they all shimmer and sparkle!

At least some birds can sense the magnetic field of the Earth, something humans need a compass to do. This is one of the many ways migrating birds are able to fly thousands of miles to find a destination we have never seen before. Homing pigeons were the first to show this to humans, who always wondered why homers could always find home, no matter where people released them.

We birds also see in finer detail than humans do. Researchers who counted the special cells in the eye responsible for seeing fine detail were flabbergasted with what they found. These cells are called cones. A human has 200,000 of them per square millimeter in the area of the eye with the most perfect vision. No one has counted a parrot's yet, but sparrows have twice the number humans do. Raptors like hawks and eagles have more than a million. No wonder an eagle can see a mouse from nearly five hundred feet away. And humans have only one area of perfect vision in the eye, called the fovea. Most of us birds have two!

Chapter Five

"Look at this, Chuck!" Yellow Crest checked her computer and gasped. "Snowball's video has gone viral! This is phenomenal!"

In fact, more and more people were watching my dance video by the hour. By the end of the first week, more than 200,000 people around the world had seen me dance!

Soon the media calls began. The producer of a TV show called *The Morning Show with Mike and Juliet* was first up. Could I fly down to New York so they could tape me dancing before their live studio audience?

Now, as you can see from my handsome physique, I'm a cockatoo in prime physical condition. As well as possessing extraordinary artistic gifts, I'm very strong and healthy. But flying from Schererville, Indiana, to New York, New York? I have to admit, that seemed an

Inspected By: Christian_Garza

00079075915

0007907

5915

c-2

L-11

awful lot to ask. That's more than seven hundred miles! Seven hundred miles of flying among hawks by day and owls by night. In the wild, I would normally fly everywhere in a flock of a hundred other cockatoos. Would I be expected to do this all alone? Though most of us birds can navigate without a compass, frankly, I wasn't even sure I'd find the way.

Yellow Crest told me not to worry. I wouldn't have to lift a wing till I got to the studio. I'd be flying by airplane—like all the stars do. Now, this was more like it! I'd never been on an airplane before. It sounded appropriately glamorous. Naturally I would sit in First Class. Maybe I should get some shades, so my fans wouldn't mob me at the airport and delay our boarding…

I was excitedly looking forward to the trip—until Yellow Crest and her mate brought out the cat carrier.

Yuck! I was supposed to ride in this thing? The carrier reminded me of the humiliating eviction from my first home. What kind of star rides around in a cat carrier? A limo would have been more appropriate. I slicked back my feathers and suppressed a hiss as I stepped in. Apparently, show biz wasn't going to be quite as glamorous as I had hoped.

I didn't get out of that carrier until hours and hours later. Finally, I had arrived: here I was in New York City, New York—arguably the world's artistic and intellectual hub, home of Broadway, Radio City Music Hall . . . and *The Morning Show*. There, I, Snowball, would make my television debut—and parrot history.

"We have a very special guest waiting in the wings—and I mean wings," said Mike, one of the hosts of my show.

"He's a global superstar, and an Internet sensation," chimed in Juliet, the other host. (I don't think they were a mated pair; I never saw them preen one another.) "You may not know Snowball now—but you will!" she promised. "He's got some pretty fly dance moves!"

Yellow Crest and I watched the TV monitor from the station's so-called Green Room. This is the room backstage where lesser guests than I are rightfully confined while they wait to go on the air. But why was I in exile? How could my show be going on without me?

Let me tell you something about us birds. Patience does not number among our many virtues. Remember, our heritage is a wild, free world where, if we want something, we can get it fast—because we can fly. In the wild, if we're bored or unhappy, we up and go where the action is.

We're not used to waiting around.

For minute after boring minute, Mike and Juliet droned on and on. What were they talking about? I'm not even sure; they were all topics that, honestly, could only possibly interest one single species on this whole planet. The other millions of species would be just as bored as I. The hosts wasted even more time interviewing other guests—mere humans!—while I was waiting to go on. Whose show did they think this was, anyway?

At least the hosts spoke of me on air before each commercial break. But it was not always in the glowing terms I deserved. Yes, they acknowledged that my dancing was sensational, all right. "But," Mike asked the audience, "is there a snowball's chance in heck he'll do it live? Tune in later and we'll find out!"

All this waiting had me pretty irritated by the time I finally took the stage. "Ladies and gentlemen," Mike announced, "please welcome . . . Snowball the Dancing Cockatoo!"

Then, I heard the sound of a rainstorm. But there was no rain. What else could be making that loud noise? As I looked out into the audience, I saw the sound was being made by hundreds and hundreds of clapping hands. A huge flock of people was out there in the audience, watching us. I had never seen so many humans. Nor had I seen such bright lights. On my T stand, I turned my back to the lights and the audience for a moment. Focus, Snowball!, I told myself. This is your big break—don't blow it!

Now I was almost ready. There was just one more thing left to do before my act, and that's what we parrots always do before any kind of athletic undertaking—like flying. You don't want to be carrying any excess baggage, no sir. When we fly, or when we dance, we need to be light as a feather. So . . . I delicately lifted up my tail and let loose a nice big poop. Ah, much better!

For some reason, the Juliet lady considered this remarkable. "Snowball is . . . going to the bathroom!" she narrated—as if the audience couldn't figure this out for themselves. Why was she so astonished? Hadn't any of their other guests pooped on air before? Juliet should try it herself—it would make her feel much better.

But this was no time for offering her tips. (For that, she could read my memoirs, once I finish dictating them.) The Backstreet Boys' "Everybody" was starting up. Yellow Crest carried me on her arm from the T stand to the back of a gold upholstered chair. My crest shot up. I bobbed once, twice, and, like a surfer catching a wave, I waited to catch the beat and ride it out. . . .

"Will he do it? I didn't see him doing much dancing in the Green Room," said Juliet anxiously. "I'm kind of concerned about this. . . ."

I wished Juliet would just go and poop already! It would really help with her anxiety problem. But now she was making me nervous. I bobbed my head a couple of times, but failed to catch the beat. So I waited and listened. *Rock your body, right!* I needed to do just this.

"C'mon, Snowball!" urged Yellow Crest. She started bobbing her head, waving her right arm. Pretty soon Mike and Juliet joined in. They were all sitting in chairs, so they looked pretty lame, truth to tell—but soon, I could tell, the audience was going to start watching them. And that wouldn't do at all!

This was my moment—and I wasn't about to let three humans trying to dance while sitting in their chairs steal my show. I threw myself into my art. Up went my crest, and then I began my dance: left foot, right foot, left, left—sway the body, step to the side . . . .

It was almost over before I knew it. Applause broke out like a rainstorm—even louder now. I tossed my crest to acknowledge my new fans and screamed with joy. This, I knew, was only the beginning.

BIRD BASICS — SAY WHAT?

Parrots and people have very different mouths, you may have noticed. We have sharp, strong, gleaming, hard beaks; and you, poor things, have these soft, flabby, floppy things called lips where your beak should be. I've heard people wonder how parrots talk with no lips, but I wonder how on earth you can talk with them!

The fact is, you and I use different structures to make the same sounds. Watch a person speak, or pay attention when you speak, and you'll see humans use the lips to make the sounds for "p," "b," and "d." But a bird can do it with a completely closed beak!

That's because we parrots can move structures in our bodies that people can't. A parrot's windpipe is flexible; a human's is not. A parrot uses the beak, tongue, glottis (the little manhole-cover-like flap that sits atop the windpipe) and esophagus (food tube) to make the sounds people make with lips.

So even though, unlike our beaks, your lips are pretty useless when you're climbing up a rope, I guess you put them to good use sometimes after all.

Chapter Six

Calls were pouring in before I even made it back to my cage at home. Who wanted the new cockatoo superstar on their TV show? It was just like the Backstreet Boys said: *Every-body!*

Before Yellow Crest could even listen to all the calls that had come in from our fans, the phone rang again. It was the producer of *Inside Edition*. Could they come film me at home? Yellow Crest got out the calendar to check my schedule. When were they thinking of doing this, she asked? "How about in half an hour?" they suggested. The crew was here before we even finished unpacking my wardrobe.

Okay, I didn't have a wardrobe . . . yet. But it was clear I was going to need one. First thing on the list would be some of those dark glasses the other Hollywood stars wear. A smoking jacket would be nice—even though we birds absolutely detest smoking (and some of my roommates at Bird Lovers Only suffer chronic lung disease from breathing secondhand smoke from previous owners). Still, I knew the jacket would look great on me during photo shoots of me relaxing at home—even though, with my hectic schedule, relaxing moments were going to be few. And I'd probably need to get fitted for a tux soon, to accept my eventual Emmy.

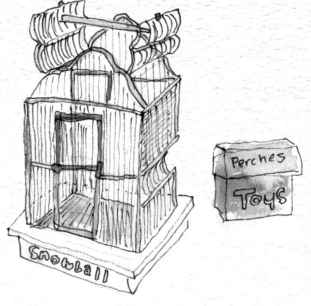

Martha Stewart called. Maybe she would want to do a makeover of my cage. (Though I have to admit I do a pretty good makeover myself! I can destroy a $10 parrot toy with my beak in sixty seconds—and then re-decorate the rest of the room by flinging the pieces through the bars of the cage. Maybe Martha wanted to take notes . . . .) But Yellow Crest politely told Martha to get in line. Ten other shows had already called before she did. They all wanted me.

The Tonight Show. The Late Show. Good Morning America. The Ellen DeGeneres Show. I danced on them all. I logged more frequent flyer miles than a migrating albatross!

And let me tell you, the celebrity life isn't nearly as easy as I may make it look. More than once, Yellow Crest had to tell David Letterman not to poke his finger too close to

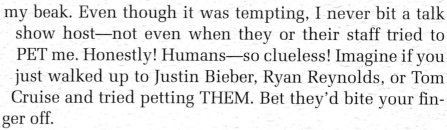

my beak. Even though it was tempting, I never bit a talk show host—not even when they or their staff tried to PET me. Honestly! Humans—so clueless! Imagine if you just walked up to Justin Bieber, Ryan Reynolds, or Tom Cruise and tried petting THEM. Bet they'd bite your finger off.

But not me. No, I was unfailingly polite—and if I do say so myself, downright helpful. I even tried to share my secret, anti-stress, weight-shedding stage tip with my fellow TV personalities. But it never caught on. When I demonstrated it to David Letterman, he didn't even notice—till I had left the stage. He found my deposit on the chair, scooped it up with a piece of paper, and followed Yellow Crest and me backstage. "You forgot something!" he called. The audience laughed at him. What a silly mistake! I didn't want it back—that was David's to keep, a souvenir from a real star!

At the end of each performance, the audience's thunderous applause made me forgive everyone their faux pas. Humans may have less common sense than we birds, but at least they have good taste in entertainment. I made a point of bowing to each host and waving goodbye to the audience before my exit.

Meanwhile, back at Bird Lovers Only, calls, letters, and emails poured in from my growing fan base all over the world. One lady wrote in from Alaska. Her mate had recently died and she was as sad as I had been when I thought mine had been eaten by an owl. But, she said, seeing my You Tube video had made her happy again. That made me happy, too. An eighth-grader wrote in from New York. Her name was Abby. She said she was my Number One fan. Her mother wrote, too, explaining she had autism. Her brain was different from most people's, a difference that made it hard for her to make friends with other kids. But she had no problems making friends with a dancing cockatoo! I let her be the head of my fan club.

It's a good thing I had Yellow Crest as my booking agent, butler, and private secretary. Although I always wrote back to Abby, I didn't have time to personally answer all my fan mail. I was busy working on new dance moves.

To provide inspiration for my genius (and because the other birds enjoy it, too), Yellow Crest and her volunteers often turned on the TV and radio in the bird rooms. This vastly expanded my musical horizons. We birds all have different tastes, as I mentioned before, and some of us like certain shows and artists and don't like others. Personally, I really clicked with fellow superstars like Michael Jackson, Queen, and Stevie Nicks (on one album cover, she poses with a cockatoo, who belongs to her brother). I enjoyed Paul McCartney, too. Smart fellow. Named his band Wings. (A far better name than his first group, which was named after a bunch of insects.) The female vocalist in a Beatlesque Chicagoland band, Jorie Gracen, sent me a CD from her group, the Pond Hawks. Though hawks, frankly, scare me to death, I loved their song "Crying Hyena." My agents recorded my endorsement as I bobbed up and down on the swivel chair in time to the bouncy beat.

But I'm a bird of many facets. My interest in music is as wide-ranging as my talents. Of course, rock, well, rocks—but I also danced to a German polka tune one of my fans mailed me on CD, to Yellow Crest's surprise. One day, I couldn't help myself, and started dancing to a television commercial. But hey, sometimes commercials are the best things on TV. Take mine, for instance: I made one for Taco Bell (ad-

vertising its new, cool, fruit-flavored drink to the tune of "The Pina Colada Song") and another for Geico (in which I danced with Geico's gecko). I even made one for a bottled water distributor in Sweden.

All this work called for new choreography. I had to come up with some major new dance moves. For the Taco Bell commercial, I ended my performance with a grand finale: I arch my back tall, spread my wings, and erect my crest while crying out an ear-splitting and triumphant *"RRRAAAAAWWWKK!"* (I love getting in the last word. It's not a word in English, but it sure is in cockatoo!) Unfortunately, the producers cut out my comment, editing for those humans who don't speak parrot, and substituted an English phrase at the end. But at least I still get the last word. For the German polka tune, I swayed from side to side, swinging my head low with my marvelous yellow crest unfurled. To Michael Jackson's "Billie Jean," I stepped rather than swayed, tossed my crest up, held it still (for my grateful photographers), then down, then back up again. In one hot new step I recently invented, I turn my head, bring my claw to my beak and, crest up, push the claw away and look in the opposite direction. It's my way of blowing kisses to the crowds, and it really rocks the house.

My agents made more videos, and put them up on You Tube. In one, I'm rocking out to "Another One Bites the Dust." In another, I do a tribute to Michael Jackson, may he rest in peace. (We put out a DVD of me dancing to some of my favorite Christmas tunes, titled "Snowball's Snowy Christmas.") Clips from my talk show appearances and commercials are all over the web, and drive traffic as well as solicit donations to www.birdloversonly.org, our parrot rescue website. The website used to get 500 hits a month. Thanks to me, it now gets more than 80,000 monthly!

And while it's humans who, with one-third more fingers than we parrots have toes, usually type in web addresses and flick the TV remote, my fans aren't confined to a single species. As it turns out, often there's someone else watching over the human's shoulder—sometimes perched ON that shoulder. Sure, I'm a hit with millions of people. But that's just one piece of my demographic. My appeal is more than multi-cultural, more than multi-national—it's multi-species as well. To my deep professional satisfaction, I discovered that, as my career took flight across the globe, other birds were starting to take notice.

BIRD BASICS — MANY MIMICS

We parrots aren't the only birds who can talk. Mockingbirds, starlings, ravens, and others can speak, too. And let's remember that birds easily find more interesting things to mimic than the human voice: The calls of insects. The songs of frogs. The whine of machinery.

The great birder and artist Roger Tory Peterson knew a mockingbird who lived by his mechanic's shop. The bird learned to imitate the sounds of all the different car motors. A male European blackbird terrorized an English neighborhood for weeks with his morning repertoire: the wail of ambulance sirens, the shriek of car alarms, and the nagging ring of cell phones—a symphony he started daily at 5 a.m. And in Australia, where a flute-playing farmer kept a lyrebird as a pet, the bird loved to sing part of the man's favorite song. When the farmer later let the lyrebird go, the bird went to work teaching others the tune. For thirty years afterwards, lyrebirds in that park were known for singing the song.

Chapter Seven

I hate to dis humans—after all, some of my best friends are humans—but an awful lot gets past them. Maybe it's because of their inferior eyesight, compared to a bird's-eye view. Maybe they are so muzzy-headed they are only dimly aware of the world of animals around them. In any case, since I'd come to town, a dance revolution was taking place in parrotdom, right under humans' big noses, and they didn't even know it! Even at our parrot rescue, not even Yellow Crest noticed—at first.

Well, I have to forgive her. Besides her main job—managing my career—Yellow Crest spends eighty hours a week tending to up to fifty of us rescued birds at a time, feeding us, cleaning our cages, organizing our entertainment. She can't be everywhere at once. So it's not her fault she didn't notice at first when Angel and I started our dance contests.

As I mentioned, at Bird Lovers Only, our human staff tries to vary our days to keep our lives interesting. After all, in the wild we'd normally be flying over miles of new territory daily, discovering different fruits and nuts, meeting different birds and other animals every day, experiencing different weather and seasons. Compared to this, just sitting in a cage in the suburbs would be so boring we'd all pull our feathers out. So the people move our cages around so we have different roommates; they give us all sorts of new toys and treats regularly; they turn on different radio shows and TV programs at different times of day.

So one day, when my cage was placed next to Angel's (she's the lock-picking Moluccan I told you about earlier), we were listening to the radio together. Both of us were perched atop our respective cages. When one song came on I particularly liked, I started doing my thing. Next thing I knew, Angel was swaying and bobbing, too.

I paused to watch her efforts. Not bad! Granted, she was no superstar like me—but who else is? Angel clearly had a respect for my art. And, lucky parrot, she had a chance to learn from the Master. After bobbing to a few bars of music, she stopped and looked to me. I showed her one of the new steps I was working on—it involved tossing my sulfur-colored crest double-time to the music. (Moluccans have salmon-colored feathers on the head, so I thought we'd have a multi-colored crest fest.) I stopped to see what she would do. She didn't try the new move, but she nodded her approval, bobbing her head up and down, up and down, up and down, bouncing her whole body. Then she paused and waited. What would I show her next? This time I demonstrated a different dance, the one I call the cocka-two-step: lift the left claw twice, the right claw once, the left claw twice, the right claw once. I paused. But Angel had a different idea: she climbed from the cage onto a rope hanging from the ceiling and twirled to the music!

Just then, over the radio, we heard the sound of human footsteps. My audience! I began to dance with even greater enthusiasm, but Angel froze. She was used to being scolded for opening cages and tossing food around. Rather than being caught in the act of dancing, she looked up at Yellow Crest with an expression that said, "Who, me?"

After that day, Angel and I held our dance competitions every time our cages were placed together and the radio was on. The other birds around us would bob their heads in time. Those who can't dance would shriek out their favorite phrases in English, parrot, or other languages. Mookie was talking in sheep, as usual—and her *"BAAAAAA"* was so loud that one day Yellow Crest managed to sneak up on us unheard.

"Angel! Snowball! What are you two doing?" she cried, laughing so hard she almost fell down. So we showed her. As the music played, Angel climbed up the rope and bobbed her head. Then she paused and looked at me. I tossed my crest and stepped high with my claws. Then it was Angel's turn. She twirled round and round on the rope. "Angel," Yellow Crest asked, "are you trying to out-do Snowball?"

Ha! Nobody would even *think* of trying that, I knew! I'm *original— Ye-ah!* The Backstreet Boys said so, after all.

We superstars accept that our role in popular culture is larger than just being entertainers. We are taste-makers as well. After all, imitation is the highest form of flattery—and parrots are great mimics. So it didn't surprise me one bit when I discovered that, thanks to me and the media blitz surrounding my inspirational talent, all around the world, parrots of all kinds—from African grays to Amazons, from little parakeets to giant Hyacinth macaws—were getting down to music ranging from Motown to Mozart.

Eventually, even their humans caught on.

"This time, 'shake a tail feather' actually involves tail feathers!" read the notice on the Internet. "Anyone who saw the viral video of Snowball the Cockatoo dancing to the Backstreet Boys is well aware that some birds can definitely bust a move." And so, the announcement continued, the Bird Channel and *Bird Talk* magazine decided to take it a step further. To showcase some of the acts I had inspired, they announced "The World's First Bird Dance-Off Contest."

The competition was fierce. Hundreds submitted videos of birds dancing. Gucci, a Hyacinth macaw, bobbed and spread his wings to Richard Barry's classic

1955 hit, "Louie, Louie." Marley, a red macaw, did a line dance to "Mariana Mambo." Ty, an African gray, swayed and sang (in high, bell-like parrot notes) to Pink's "I'm Not Here for Your Entertainment." (When I heard the lyrics "don't touch—back up," I wondered if the songwriter was a biter.)

Personally, rap isn't my thing (a blessing for which Yellow Crest, whose taste runs to folk and the Methodist church hymnal, says she is eternally grateful). But a lot of my fellow parrots dig it. Zach, a blue and gold macaw, placed as one of the twelve finalists with his rhythmic marching and side-to-side swaying to Juelz Santana's "Let Me See You Get Low"—whose only musical accompaniment was whistling and percussion. Possibly Mr. Santana had gotten his inspiration from a cockatiel. Tikki, a Goffin's cockatoo, hopped to the beat of another rap song, swaggering with extended wings as he marched and strutted all over the floor.

Yellow Crest and I followed the contest closely, since I'd been the inspiration for it and all. I'd sit on her shoulder as she'd check BirdChannel.com to watch the videos posted on the web. One hundred thousand visitors to the website voted on the finalists! According to contest rules, birds were judged on their dance style, rhythm, and creativity—the very attributes, of course, that make my own work so brilliant. I set the bar—or should we call it a T stand?—very high indeed.

Which bird, we wondered, would prove worthy of my rock 'n' roll legacy? Would it be the line-dancing macaw? A head-banging Goffin's? A be-bopping budgie? A hip-hop rapper like Tikki or Zach?

On the Internet, viewers' comments on the dancers were flying as thick and fast as a swirling flock of blackbirds. As the votes flooded in, the excitement built. I have to admit I felt a twinge—just a twinge—of concern when I read this post on the web: "Who among these talented parrots," one viewer wondered, "will be the next Snowball?"

The NEXT Snowball? What about the ACTUAL Snowball? The CURRENT Snowball? The one and only REAL Snowball? Were the humans forgetting who had started this whole rock 'n' roll craze in the first place? Could my genius be eclipsed by some fly-by-night impostor?

Of course, I shouldn't have worried. No one could touch my creds as the hottest rocker in all of parrotdom. Nobody was treading on my tail feathers. The Grand Champion, as it happened, was a stand-out in more ways than one: the title went to Poirot, a Congo African gray belonging to Mother Barbara of the Convent of St. Elizabeth in Etna, California. Holding a silver spoon in one claw and waving it like a queen's scepter, Poirot performed a delicate ballet to classical composer Antonio Vivaldi's 1723 violin concerto "The Four Seasons."

BIRD BASICS — LIVING DINOSAURS

Who are the mightiest beasts who ever lived on Earth? The dinosaurs, you might say—adding that it's too bad that they're extinct. Except you'd be wrong. Mighty they were. Extinct they're not. And I should know. I'm one of them!

In fact, you might have seen a dinosaur at your bird feeder today. You might have eaten one for Thanksgiving supper! Most scientists agree the dinosaurs are actually alive and thriving—in the forms of the ten thousand species of living birds, from hummingbirds to ostriches to parrots like me.

Today there's lots of evidence that birds are dinosaurs' living descendants. Many dinosaurs had feathers. Lots of them had beaks. And many of them—especially the fastest, smartest dinosaurs, meat-eaters like Velociraptor—had adaptations that would later be essential for flight, like swiveling wrists and big, forward-facing eyes. Lots of the early bird-like dinosaurs had long arms that could be folded against the body, as birds' wings are today. Large hands with three long fingers eventually evolved into the tips of wings, and long tails turned into aerodynamic rudders for gliding.

Loads of new fossils show links between birds and dinosaurs. Many baby dinosaurs hatched out of their eggs covered in down like most of us birds do as babies today. Fossils discovered in China showed many species of dinosaurs had wings (some had four of them! Two on the arms and two on the legs. Now that would be great!). But some of the most convincing evidence comes from a scientist who was able to find not just fossilized bones, but actually soft tissue, almost miraculously preserved, from a Tyrannosaurus Rex. Using her sample, she was able to look at some of the genetic blueprints for this most ancient and formidable dinosaur. What living creature did the blueprints most resemble? Barnyard poultry—suggesting that T. Rex might have tasted like chicken.

Chapter Eight

One day, Yellow Crest announced I'd be meeting a new visitor. Naturally, by this time I was a seasoned pro, used to the usual fans, the paparazzi, the film crews. I was a regular guest on the talk shows. There was also, of course, my commercial work; and my great good looks were often sought after by still photographers around the world. But this visitor was different. His name was Ani Patel and he had come from a place called the Neurosciences Institute. Yellow Crest was excited.

That he had flown halfway across the country, from California, just to see me didn't particularly impress me. After all, no fewer than four film crews had already come from Japan to film me. But because my favorite human seemed thrilled he had come, I was intrigued. I know that humans (poor things!) can't erect their hair as well as we do our feathers, but it seemed to me her crest rose a little higher the moment he walked in.

Why? I wondered. Yellow Crest already had a mate, so that wasn't the attraction. Had they been nestlings together? Was he a long-lost flock mate? No, that wasn't it, either. Finally Yellow Crest explained why she was so excited: This fellow was a scientist. He had come so I could teach him about music and the brain.

Ah! Well, let's get right to work then, I thought. He'd come to the right place. I was happy to help. It was about time that people learned a thing or two about brains, and I, Sir Snowball, was just the one to explain it all.

See, when it comes to the study of brains, humans (as usual!) have everything all mixed up. The first thing they need to get straight is that size doesn't matter. People are always going on and on about their big brains. (Some of them have the bad manners to mention, in the same breath, the fact that a parrot's brain is about the size of a shelled walnut.) Well, so what? Anything can be miniaturized.

Just think of computers. They started out as machines that took up a whole room for just one. Now you can fit one in your pocket.

And another thing people don't seem to understand . . .

Rock your bo-dy!

I'll save that brilliant thought for later, I figured. Yellow Crest had started up the CD player, and I just couldn't resist dancing. I was feeling particularly peppy that day, and threw in some of my newest moves. My repertoire now included a head-banging dance like those popular at punk rock clubs. I also threw in my show-stopper, that move when I throw kisses to the crowd with my claw. I tossed my crest graciously as my small but enthusiastic audience cried "Yay, Snowball!" and clapped in appreciation.

"Wow!" said the Patel fellow when I had finished. "He really does seem to sync to the beat! I've never known any species but humans could do that before!"

I might be more original than the Backstreet Boys even imagined! But what Ani Patel said made perfect sense to me. I know a thing or two about the other species, after all. (Even though I don't fly free, I do travel quite a bit, plus I enjoy the wildlife specials on TV.) I've noticed that chimpanzees sometimes do a sort of dance when it's raining hard, jumping and swinging as if riding the energy of the storm. Dolphins sure bust a move when they leap high out of the water. Some of them even spin around in the air—even better than Angel does on her rope during our contests! Even bees can dance. They do so to tell each other where the best flowers are.

That's different, though, than dancing TO THE RHYTHM of a song. When I get down, in sync with the beat, I'm doing something more complicated than what these other animals do. This Patel fellow clearly appreciated that. He explained it all to Yellow Crest:

"What Snowball is doing is quite complex," he said. "First, Snowball's brain has to recognize that the beat of the song is a pattern. Then he has to figure out what that pattern is. He has to produce a mental model of the song's beat in his brain. And finally, he has to get his body to coordinate with the rhythm in his head. This bird is really impressive!"

At the Neurosciences Institute, Ani Patel had been studying how humans respond to music for many years. He had thought that only human brains were sophisticated enough to appreciate the arts of music, language, and dance. Now, because of me, he was starting to realize he might have been wrong. Parrots might be smarter than people ever suspected.

Well, duh!

Humans love to crow that they're the only species to do this or do that. "Humans are the only species to use tools," they used to claim—until the scientist Jane Goodall noticed chimps using special probes they had fashioned from sticks to pry termites out of nests. "Humans are the only species that have language," they used to say. Parrots quickly put an end to THAT idea!

Why are humans so obsessed with proving they're unique? ALL species are unique, seems to me—just like every individual. (Though some individuals, if I do say so myself, are more unique than others.) I guess the people are trying to make up for their embarrassing lack of talent in other departments. They're slow runners, they can hardly swim, and they can't fly at all. Pathetic!

Even though the superiority of my parrot brain was obvious, Ani Patel still wanted to test it. You know how scientists are. They love to come up with new ideas—they call them hypotheses—and then test them over and over to see if they're right or wrong. I was going to be part of his science project.

"Do you think he would still dance in sync," he asked Yellow Crest, "if we changed the song's tempo?" He wanted to see whether I could change the way I danced to keep up with the beat at a new speed.

"I don't know," said Yellow Crest. "Let's find out."

So that's what they did. Ani used a machine to create eleven different versions of my favorite song—same lyrics, same tune, but he changed the tempo. In some versions, the song was faster. In some versions, it was slower. Then there were versions that were REALLY slow. Bor-ing! I didn't like those at all. Nobody wants to slow dance to a rock song!

Over the course of many weeks, Yellow Crest and her mate filmed me dancing to the different versions of the song. Ani Patel told them they weren't even allowed to dance with me while they were filming. That took resolve—it's almost impossible not to dance when I'm rockin' the joint! But Ani was firm on this. He thought the humans might be giving me cues to the beat. Ha! Little did he know that it's ME who usually gives the cues around here. After all, I'm always the lead dancer.

Yellow Crest sent the films off to California. I knew I'd make it to Hollywood! Actually they were in a place called San Diego, but I'm sure that's nearby. There, lucky Ani Patel and his staff got to watch me dance for hours and hours, over and over—even in slow motion! They slowed the videos down to sixty frames per second, so they wouldn't miss a thing.

They concluded that, yes, I really was dancing to the beat. Yes, I really could change my dance to match the music. And it really rocked the world of science. My feat was headline news from New York to LA, from Tokyo to Sydney, Australia. A PARROT can sync to music! Humans aren't the only ones who can dance!

I tried to explain what all the fuss was about to my flock mates here at the parrot rescue. Mookie listened carefully, squinted his eyes at me, scratched his head with his foot, fluffed up his feathers, and said, *"So?"*

Angel's reaction: *"Well, duh!"*

I think I liked Ben's comment best of all: *"Pfffftttttttttthhhhh!"*

Humans! I still have so much to teach them.

BIRD BASICS — BRAINY BIRDS

Once upon a time, certain people considered someone who wasn't very smart a "bird brain." But not since a parrot named Alex spoke up.

Alex was an ordinary pet store parrot—an African gray like Mitzi, Ben or Bandit—when researcher Irene Pepperberg brought him to her scientific laboratory. At a time when other scientists were investigating whether chimps and dolphins could use sign language, Dr. Pepperberg quite reasonably chose to work with someone who could actually speak. Alex learned to use more than one hundred words. And he used them just like you would: to answer questions ("What color is this, Alex? What shape? What's it made from?"), make requests ("Wanna nut! Wanna shower! Come here!"), and express emotions (including "I'm sorry!" when he'd been bad). Alex learned to count to eight and, without a single arithmetic lesson, even figured out how to add.

Alex died unexpectedly at the young age of thirty-one in 2007. In his last words, spoken the night before he was found dead on the bottom of his cage, he told his scientific collaborator and best friend, Dr. Pepperberg, "See you tomorrow. I love you." Though, alas, his life was too brief, his impact was lasting. This parrot changed forever what people think of how birds think. It turns out our minds are remarkably alike.

Chapter Nine

Ah! I love mornings. All parrots do. When the first rays of light start streaming in the windows of the parrot rescue, our birdy spirits rise with the sun. We can't help but start singing—and talking, and screaming—to welcome the new day. We're excited about our coming schedule: of delicious food, visits with human and parrot friends, climbing on play gyms, watching educational TV, listening to CDs and radio—and often, for me, basking in the warm glow of another spotlight and the splendid rainstorm sound of applause from a grateful audience.

This particular morning was extra-special. Yellow Crest made me my favorite breakfast—blueberry waffles and scrambled eggs (not parrot eggs, mind you!)—just to keep up my strength. I had a gig with *Animal Planet*. Another opening, another show.

I'd been on *Animal Planet* before, but today's filming would be different. "Snowball, we have a new assignment," Yellow Crest told me. "Today, you're going to be a teacher!"

A teacher! Wait a minute—I already have a job, I thought. I'm an international superstar. An Internet sensation. Hero of stage and screen. My rightful place is in front of a camera, not in front of a classroom!

But then Yellow Crest promised me that *Animal Planet* planned for me to do both: The idea was to film me teaching children how to dance at one of Chicago's dance studios. I'd be on camera the whole time.

Ah. That might be all right then. And, really, who could blame the young humans for wanting to learn from an idol? Who was I, Sir Snowball, to deny them the opportunity to study under a Master? The French have a saying that I learned from TV: *noblesse oblige*. Nobility obliges: it's the obligation of those of us of high status to be honorable and generous. And, as said Marcus Cicero, the first-century-BC Roman philosopher and orator (another guy I met on educational TV): "What nobler employment, or more valuable to the state," he asked, "than that of the parrot who instructs the rising generation?"

(At least that's how I remembered it. A lot of other birds were screaming during that particular sentence.) Cicero was a cool guy. Talented and famous, like me—and not bad looking for someone with no feathers, judging from all the marble busts and statues state artists made to celebrate him. (Note to self: remind Yellow Crest to schedule sculptor.)

I decided to go along with it. So, I wondered, when would *Animal Planet* be sending my limo?

But, alas. The next thing I knew, Yellow Crest's mate was stuffing my favorite dancing chair into the back of the car . . . and out came the cat carrier. Oh, well. *Noblesse oblige.*

At the studio, the people placed my chair in the front of a big room. The studio had wooden perches along the walls, and floor-to-ceiling mirrors on all sides. Everywhere I looked, there I was! Great décor, I thought. (Note to self: remind Yellow Crest to phone interior decorator for home make-over.)

The splendid views I was getting were soon interrupted, though. About a dozen girls—little ones maybe only five years old, middle-sized ones, and others who were teenagers—filed into the room wearing their colorful dance togs. My students. My crest went up as I eyed them thoughtfully.

Their regular dance instructor, a human, introduced me to the class. "This is Snowball," she said. "He's going to be your teacher today." The children began to murmur in excitement. Some giggled. They'd never had a teacher who was a cockatoo before. I was going to rock their socks off.

"What we're going to do," said the human teacher, "is, Snowball will show you a dance, and you're supposed to copy it, okay?"

More murmurs. I don't blame them for worrying. How can you copy genius? Of course, none of them could hope to be as graceful or talented as me. First of all, they were missing much of the equipment. I've already mentioned humans' pathetic lack of wings and feathers. Second, some of them were just fledglings. The little ones were going to have a hard time at this.

So I tried to go easy on them. I'd start with my easiest dance move: the cocka-two step. The instructor slipped the Backstreet Boys' CD into the player. The crew started filming. Okay, girls, like this: Crests up, ladies! Now, right claw once, left claw twice. Right claw once, left claw twice . . .

The beat was carrying me up and down, up and down. The cameras were rolling, the lights bright. This teaching thing was fun—and easy! Maybe I should consider starting a dance academy, like Fred Astaire did: "Learn the Steps of a Star at Snowball's School of Dance." Note to self . . .

But wait! All of a sudden I realized something was wrong—dreadfully wrong! Many of the older girls were, given their human limitations, doing a reasonable job of copying me. But some of the younger girls were WAY off. One of them was twirling like a ballerina. Another one was doing the twist. The littlest girl was just stamping her feet and waving her arms. They weren't following me at all!

I stopped mid-move on my chair. I stared at my students sternly. My crest went down. What was the matter with them?

And then something really horrible happened.

The cameraman swung his lens away from me. Instead, he was focusing on the littlest girl. She was giggling and prancing, and flapping her arms like a fledgling just out of the nest. She wasn't even doing the dance right!

In public, I tend to express myself with dance rather than with human speech. But this time, I couldn't help myself. At the top of my parrot lungs, I yelled out a phrase I had learned from my first true love. She used to yell it a lot at her parents when she was a teenager:

"IT'S NOT FAIR! IT'S NOT FAIR!!!"

Post Script

The film crew saw the error of their ways. Though they continued to film my efforts to teach the young humans that day, the little girl ended up on the cutting room floor. When "Animal Planet's Most Outrageous Animals" finally aired, it included no footage of any of my students at all. Though the producer did keep that great shot of me on the dancing chair in the studio surrounded by perches and mirrors. Smart choice!

I rather regret the incident with my youngest student. After all, it wasn't the cameraman's fault he swung away to look at her. He was probably just rubbernecking, the way you can't help but look at a car accident on the highway. And it wasn't the little girl's fault she couldn't copy me. Nobody can dance like Snowball the Dancing Cockatoo—except Snowball the Dancing Cockatoo, of course!

So I've put a stop to my plans for Snowball's School of Dance for the moment. No matter. My days are very busy. My calendar is full to bursting. Good thing Yellow Crest keeps track of my schedule.

I'm working on new dance videos—sales of my DVDs, available at www.birdloversonly.org, benefit my parrot rescue. And, of course, as befits a celeb of my stature, there's my charity work for people. Most recently, I staged an appearance at a dance-a-thon to raise money for needy children in southwest Indiana.

I have a number of other projects in mind. But I also want to keep some flexibility in my busy schedule. You never know. Who can guess what new adventures might await me? One thing's for sure: I'll certainly be in demand to help the humans. They need all the help they can get.

The End

Afterword

Snowball lives at Bird Lovers Only, which is a not-for-profit, donation-based rescue service for unwanted, abused, and special needs parrots. Bird Lovers Only relies on charitable support so that it can continue to conduct music cognition studies with Snowball, to assist in finding new homes for parrots, and to educate the public on parrot intelligence.

  Want to support its work? Write to Snowball and his friends at the address below, or visit the website at:

www.birdloversonly.org

Bird Lovers Only
560 Pond View Drive
Duncan, S.C. 29334

Here are links to internet videos referred to in the text:

p. 7   www.metacafe.com/watch/1162323/parrot_dancing_snowball_the_cockatoo/
p. 20 www.youtube.com/watch?v=N7IZmRnAo6s
p. 31 www.youtube.com/watch?v=6fAVRDezNhs
p. 37 www.youtube.com/watch?v=A4E6HOPtU90
p. 45 www.birdchannel.com/bird-magazines/bird-talk/Bird_Dance_Off_Finalists_result.aspx
p. 52 www.cbsnews.com/video/watch/?id=6554351n
p. 59 www.youtube.com/watch?v=OHq4bYJbsBs
       For lots of other videos of Snowball, go to the You Tube channel: Bird Lovers Only Rescue

Useful information:

Sy Montgomery's website: www.symontgomery.com
Judith Oksner's website: www.judithoksner.com
Great site for all things "bird": http://www.birdchannel.com
World Parrot Trust: www.parrots.org

Other Books for Children by Sy Montgomery:

Temple Grandin: How the Woman Who Loved Cows Embraced Autism and Changed the World
Kakapo Rescue: Saving the World's Strangest Parrot
Saving the Ghost of the Mountain: An Expedition Among Snow Leopards in Mongolia
Quest for the Tree Kangaroo: An Expedition to the Cloud Forest of New Guinea
Search for the Golden Moon Bear
The Tarantula Scientist
Encantado: Pink Dolphin of the Amazon
The Man-Eating Tigers of Sundarbans
The Snake Scientist

To research books, films and articles, *Sy Montgomery* has been chased by an angry silverback gorilla in Zaire and bitten by a vampire bat in Costa Rica, worked in a pit crawling with 18,000 snakes in Manitoba, and handled a wild tarantula in French Guiana. She has been deftly undressed by an orangutan in Borneo, hunted by a tiger in India, and swum with piranhas, electric eels, and dolphins in the Amazon.

Sy's work has been honored with many awards, including the Robert F. Sibert Informational Book Medal and the American Association for the Advancement of Science's Book and Film Prize. She writes for both adults and children. *Snowball* is her tenth book for kids.

Sy lives in Hancock, New Hampshire with her husband, the writer Howard Mansfield, Sally, their Border Collie, and ten hens.

Judith Oksner has taught for many years at all levels from elementary grades through high school, and at the same time, continued a lifelong passion for painting. She studied liberal and fine arts in college and

in graduate school and over time converted from a full-time teacher with a side career in art to a full-time painter with continued work in education.

She has had many exhibitions in New England and New York art galleries and has done illustrations for magazines, books, and informational reports. She is currently working on a K-12 curriculum development project for Pearson Publishing and is also at work illustrating three books—on museum art for reluctant viewers, mindfulness exercises to reduce stress in children, and a "memoir" of a Newfoundland dog and her pups.

On the side she is a constant dieter and a poor but enthusiastic recorder and bridge player. She has a wonderful husband with the forbearance of a saint, two fine sons and two totally unspoiled dogs.

Sy and Judith would like to thank the following folks for their help with this book: Jody Simpson; Martin Kerner; Sy's mate, Howard Mansfield; Judith's mate, Robert Oksner; their fledglings, Thomas and William; Yellow Crest (Irena Schulz); her mate, Chuck Schulz; and their fledgling, Danny.

ISBN 978-0-87233-156-3

Library of Congress Cataloging-in-Publication Data
Montgomery, Sy.
 Snowball the dancing cockatoo / written by Sy Montgomery ; illustrated by Judith Oksner.
    pages cm
 Audience: 8-13.
 Audience: Grade 3 to 8.
 Includes bibliographical references and index.
 ISBN 978-0-87233-156-3 (alk. paper)
1. Cockatoos--Juvenile literature. 2. Talking birds--Juvenile literature. I. Oksner, Judith, illustrator. II. Title.
 QL696.P7M795 2013
 598.7'1--dc23
                        2012049356

BAUHAN
PUBLISHING LLC
PO BOX 117 PETERBOROUGH NEW HAMPSHIRE 03458
WWW.BAUHANPUBLISHING.COM
603-567-4430

Book design by Sarah Bauhan
Cover design by Henry James
The text of this book is set in Melior.

Manufactured by Thomson-Shore, Dexter, Michigan (USA); RMA705KJ133, February, 2013

This book is also available as an enhanced ebook and has been included in the Third Grade Curriculum published by Pearson Education: www.pearsonschool.com.